for Autumn 2007!

G000127478

Includes 4 cars & dolls!

Pollywheels 4 Pack

Pollywheels

Pollywheels Micro Cars

4 pets included

Real rooted hair to style!

Paw Spa

Wild Ride Jeep

Cool new sparkle glam finish

1 Jeep, 2 dolls & pets included

Change Polly's hair, nails & make up!

Glitz 'n' Glam

Polly Sparkle House

3 ways to colour change

Secret storage area

Fashion, glitter stickers & more!

Stylin' Polly

Over 40 play pieces

Contents

polly pocket™

Published by Pedigree Books Limited,
Beech Hill House, Walnut Gardens, Exeter, Devon, EX4 4DH.
Email: books@pedigreegroup.co.uk

Pedigree®

MATTEL

polly pocket™

polly pocket™

£6.99

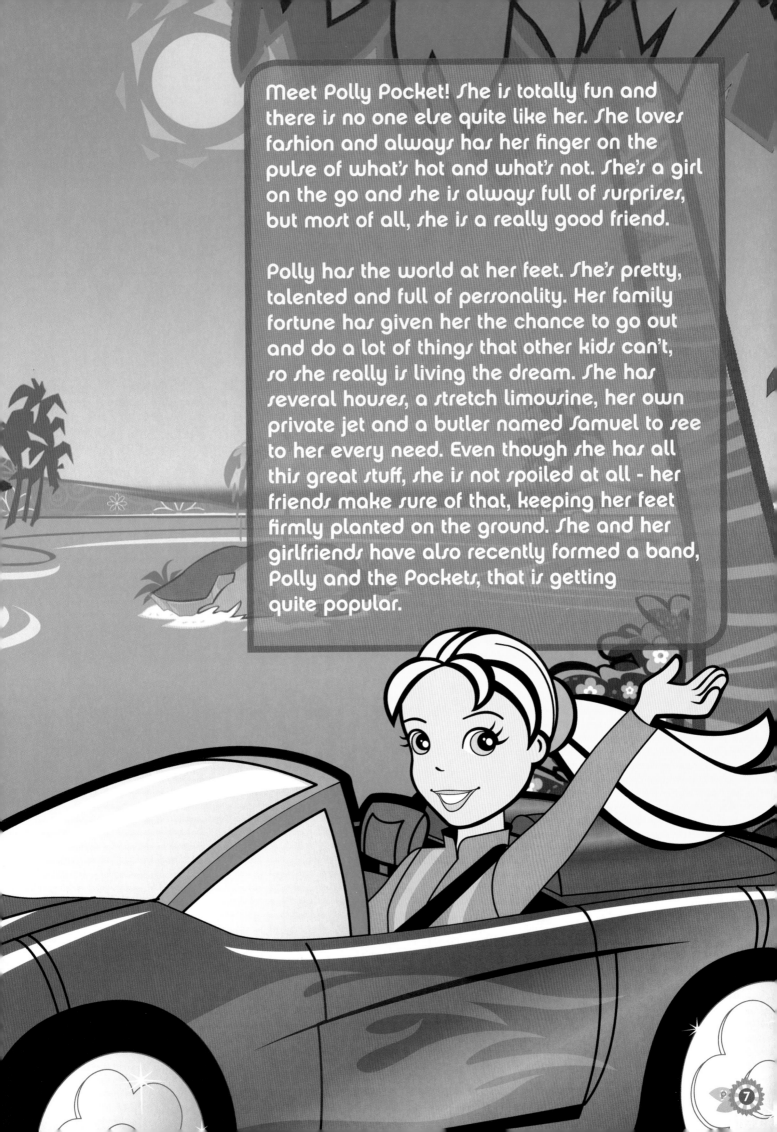

Meet Polly Pocket! She is totally fun and there is no one else quite like her. She loves fashion and always has her finger on the pulse of what's hot and what's not. She's a girl on the go and she is always full of surprises, but most of all, she is a really good friend.

Polly has the world at her feet. She's pretty, talented and full of personality. Her family fortune has given her the chance to go out and do a lot of things that other kids can't, so she really is living the dream. She has several houses, a stretch limousine, her own private jet and a butler named Samuel to see to her every need. Even though she has all this great stuff, she is not spoiled at all - her friends make sure of that, keeping her feet firmly planted on the ground. She and her girlfriends have also recently formed a band, Polly and the Pockets, that is getting quite popular.

Meet Lila...

Lila and Polly have been the best of friends ever since they met on their first day of school. Even though they are very different, they are still best buds. Lila is a brunette and is slightly less confident than Polly. Despite this, she is always in the know, trendy and chatty. She is the ultimate girly girl and loves everything feminine. Lila loves to read up on all the latest fashion trends and prides herself on knowing what and who are hot this season!

Meet Shani...

Shani is a totally cool, hip, sassy brunette, Shani is African American and plays the drums in Polly's band. Shani is really a very talented musician, she is fresh and funky and a real individual. She sometimes has a tendency to stick her nose into other peoples business, which sometimes gets her into a bit of trouble. She is really streetwise but she is also really funny with a great sense of humour.

Meet Rick...

Rick is one of Polly's closest friends. All the girls in school have a real crush on Rick, but that's not all that surprising. He's blonde, blue eyed, cool, fun and a terrific athlete. He's an all-around great guy and a master at practical jokes. All the guys at school like him and all the girls at school would like to be his girlfriend.

Meet lea...

Lea is one of Polly's best friends, she is a real outdoors type of girl who just loves to go on adventures. She is a little bit shy, but she is very smart. She is also really mischievous and loves to have fun. Whenever there is a challenge put in front of her, Lea will rise to the top and overcome it. She always says what she thinks but she never means to upset anyone. She has a bright wit to match her bright red hair and a laugh you can hear right down the block!

Polly & the Pockets On Tour!

"Hey guys!" cried Polly as she ran into the rehearsal studio, "Guess what?" "What is it Polly?" asked Lila "My Dad has totally scored us a huge gig at a concert in London!" screamed Polly!

"No way!" all the girls screamed in unison!

Polly And The Pockets had only started the band recently so for them to get a big gig in London was totally huge! "When is the gig?" asked Shani. "Well, that's the only thing," said Polly, "It's tomorrow!" "Tomorrow!" cried the girls.

"Yeah" said Polly, "I know it is really short notice but Dad says we can use the Jet to fly over. So we should get there on time but we need to leave in like, an hour!" "Wow Polly," said Shani, "That sounds great!" "I know," said Polly, "I am so excited!"

Not everyone looked excited though, Lea had been sitting quietly in the corner and had not really reacted to the news at all. Polly noticed that her friend was being unusually quiet and went over to sit next to her. "What's wrong Lea?" Polly asked. "I don't think I will be able to go," said Lea.

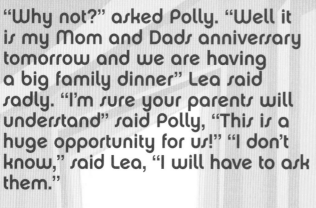

"Why not?" asked Polly. "Well it is my Mom and Dads anniversary tomorrow and we are having a big family dinner" Lea said sadly. "I'm sure your parents will understand" said Polly, "This is a huge opportunity for us!" "I don't know," said Lea, "I will have to ask them."

Shani and Lila noticed that Polly and Lea were talking in the corner of the studio and went over to see what was wrong.

"Hey girl," said Shani, "What's up?" "Lea might not be able to come with us," said Polly, "She is meant to be having a big family dinner tomorrow." "No way!" cried Shani, "So we need you to play with us!" "Yeah!" chimed in Lila, "We won't be able to do it without you!" "Come on guys," said Polly, "Lea is going to ask her parents, but we have to respect their decision." "You're right," said Shani, "Sorry Lea, I just really want you to be there with us, it would be totally sucky without you!"

Just then, Crissy walked in. "Hey girls, what's going on?" Polly explained to Crissy about the gig in London and about Lea maybe not being able to play. "Well," said Crissy, "First things first, Lea and I will go see her Mom and Dad and work out if she is going to be able to make it. You guys pack up all the instruments and we will meet you at the airport."

Polly, Shani and Lila packed all their instruments into Polly's car and headed off to the airport. They hadn't been there long when Crissy pulled up in her car. "Crissy!" cried Shani, "Where is Lea?" "Her parents said she couldn't come!" said Crissy, looking quite upset! "What are we going to do without her, she would have so loved to have come with us?!" asked Lila. "Listen girls," said Polly, "It's a total shame that Lea can't come with us, but we are just going to have to pull together as a team and make it through this!" "Polly is right" said Crissy, "Come on guys, cheer up! We're off to London!"

The girls all boarded Polly's jet and settled in for the long flight. Crissy had brought a book with her that was full of facts about London and after a while she decided it would be fun to tell the girls all about their destination. "Hey guys, did you know that the Queen of England lives in London in a place called Buckingham Palace?" asked Crissy. "And did you also know that some of the most famous bands in the world come from England?" "Really?" said the girls. "Yeah!" replied Crissy, "And there is a tower called Big Ben which isn't actually called Big Ben, Big Ben is the name of a bell inside the tower!"

"Wow Crissy," said Polly, "What else does the book say?" "Well there are totally lots of really cool things to see and do!" Crissy continued, "There is Carnaby Street, which is great for shopping, and there are the London Dungeons!" "What happened there?" asked Shani. "Well it says in here that in the olden days all the criminals in London were locked up down there!" said Crissy reading from her book, "Apparently it is pretty scary and people say there are even ghosts in there!" "I don't think I want to go there!" laughed Polly.

Soon enough the girls were flying in over London. "Look down there!" cried Crissy, "That's the Houses Of Parliament, where all the politicians make laws and stuff!" "Wow!" said Polly, "It looks like a really old building!" "What is that river called?" asked Shani. "That's the River Thames," Crissy answered, "And it runs right through the middle of London.

"This is your Captain speaking," came a voice over the plane PA system, "We will be landing in London in five minutes, so if you could all take your seats and fasten your seatbelts, that would be great."

"Excellent!" cried the girls as the settled back into their seats for landing! Soon the girls were getting off the pane and collecting their bags from the baggage collection. "Right girls!" said Polly, "What should we do first?"

After the girls had checked into their hotel, they all met in the lobby to decide what to do for the rest of the day. "I know!" said Polly, "Let's go to Buckingham Palace and see The Changing Of The Guard!" "What's that?" asked Shani. "Let me take this one Polly!" said Crissy opening up her ever trusty guidebook. "The changing of the guards is when the Queens soldiers swap over with a new shift, it's quite a big ceremony." "Ok, cool. Let's go!" said Shani.

The girls jumped into a black London cab and headed off to Buckingham Palace. "I wish that Lea was here," said Crissy as they rode in the cab. "So do I," said Polly.

Soon the girls pulled up outside Buckingham Palace. There was a really big crowd of people all gathered there to see the guards. The guards looked kind of funny with their bright red uniforms and big tall fluffy hats. As the girls stood there a grand golden carriage rolled by, being pulled by two beautiful horses. "Who's that?" asked Shani. "That's the Queen of England!" said Polly. All the girls began to wave at the carriage, and would you believe it, the Queen waved right back! "Wow!" said Polly, "Lea is totally not going to believe the Queen waved at us!"

Next the girls headed to the world famous waxworks museum. There were lots of models of famous people and the girls got to stand next to them and have their photos taken. "Lea would have enjoyed this so much!" said Shani. "I know," said Lila, "I do so wish she was here." Polly overheard her two friends and popped around the corner to make a call on her phone. Lila and Shani noticed Polly had disappeared and went off to find her. Soon they saw her heading back towards them. "Sorry guys," said Polly, "I had to make a call." "Was it important?" asked Shani. "Errm, not really," said Polly nervously, "I was just checking what time we had to be at the gig, we should really get going!" "Really?" asked Shani, "I thought the show wasn't until tonight." "Yes that's right but we have to do sound checks and have a rehearsal first" said Polly.
"And we need to work out how we are going to play the songs without Lea," said Crissy.

"Ok then guys, let's rock out of here!" said Shani.

The girls made their way to the stadium where they would be playing that night. Polly's Dad was there to meet them. "Hey Mr. Pocket!" cried Shani, "Thanks so much for arranging this show!" "It's not a problem girls, I am really looking forward to it. Wait a second, aren't you missing someone?" asked Mr. Pocket. "Yeah Dad," said Polly, "Lea couldn't make it at such short notice, she had a family dinner she had to go to." "Oh that's a shame" said Mr. Pocket, "I'm sure you guys will still do just great though." "Well that is why we came over a little early" explained Polly, "We're going to have a practice now and see how it goes." "That sounds like a very good idea Polly, good thinking," her Dad replied.

The girls climbed onto the stage and took their places. "Ok girls" yelled Polly, "Hit it!" Shani started banging away on the drums while Crissy and Lila picked up their instruments and started playing away. Polly started to sing but when she looked out into the arena she saw her Dad with an odd look on his face. "Wait a minute guys!" yelled Polly, "Dad, what's wrong?" "Well girls, it just sounds like you are missing something," said Mr. Pocket. "It's Lea, I knew we couldn't play without her!" cried Shani. "Shani's right Polly," said Crissy, " What are we going to do, the show starts in an hour and we are going to totally bomb!"

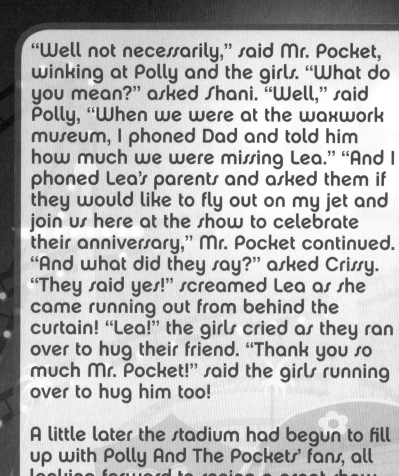

"Well not necessarily," said Mr. Pocket, winking at Polly and the girls. "What do you mean?" asked Shani. "Well," said Polly, "When we were at the waxwork museum, I phoned Dad and told him how much we were missing Lea." "And I phoned Lea's parents and asked them if they would like to fly out on my jet and join us here at the show to celebrate their anniversary," Mr. Pocket continued. "And what did they say?" asked Crissy. "They said yes!" screamed Lea as she came running out from behind the curtain! "Lea!" the girls cried as they ran over to hug their friend. "Thank you so much Mr. Pocket!" said the girls running over to hug him too!

A little later the stadium had begun to fill up with Polly And The Pockets' fans, all looking forward to seeing a great show. As the curtain opened, Polly walked to the front of the stage and hushed the crowd. "Hey guys, thanks so much for coming out to see us," Polly started, "We want to dedicate this first song to two very special people who are celebrating their wedding anniversary today, Lea's Mom and Dad!"

The whole crowd cheered and Lea's parents looked so proud. Polly And The Pockets played a great show that night, the best they had ever played.

The Holiday Poem

When Polly and her friends,
Go on a holiday,
They all enjoy themselves
In their own individual way.

Take Lila for example,
She loves to go out and shop,
Finding brand new fashions
To make all her friends jaws drop.

She'll go out to the markets,
Or fancy little boutiques
She'd like to shop forever,
For weeks and weeks
and weeks.

Then there is Shani,
Who also likes to shop,
But she's looking for music,
Like rock, or dance, or pop.

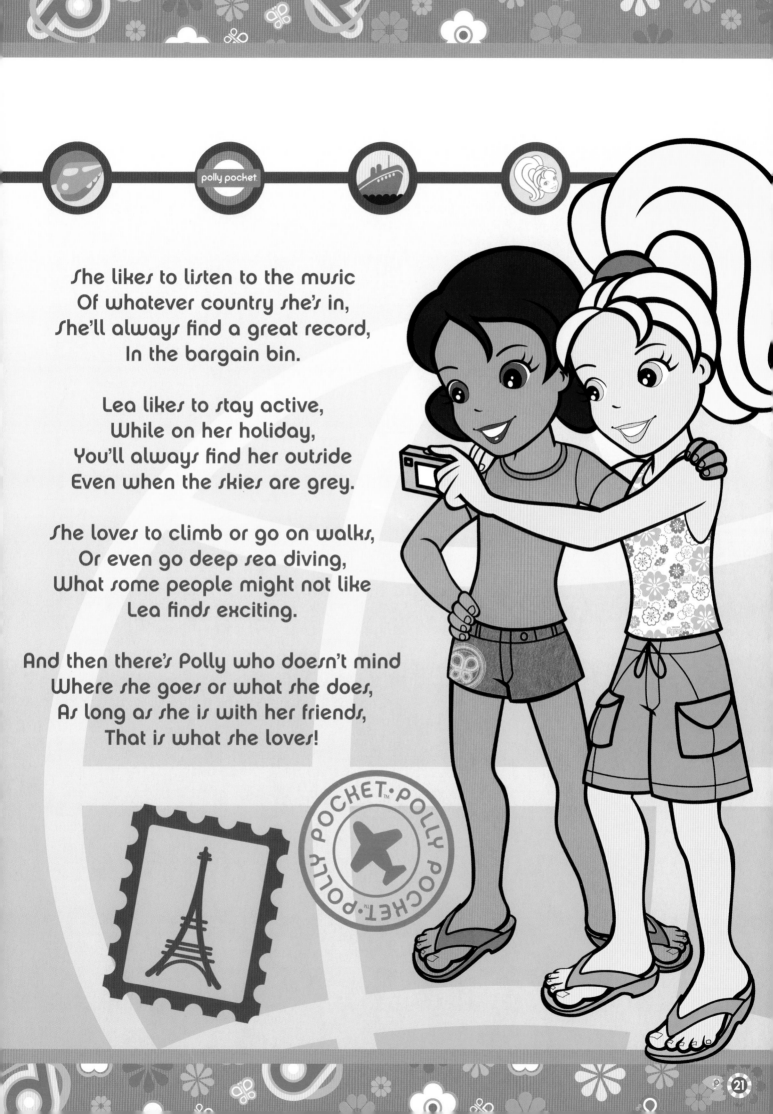

She likes to listen to the music
Of whatever country she's in,
She'll always find a great record,
In the bargain bin.

Lea likes to stay active,
While on her holiday,
You'll always find her outside
Even when the skies are grey.

She loves to climb or go on walks,
Or even go deep sea diving,
What some people might not like
Lea finds exciting.

And then there's Polly who doesn't mind
Where she goes or what she does,
As long as she is with her friends,
That is what she loves!

Polly And Friends

World Wide Colour In

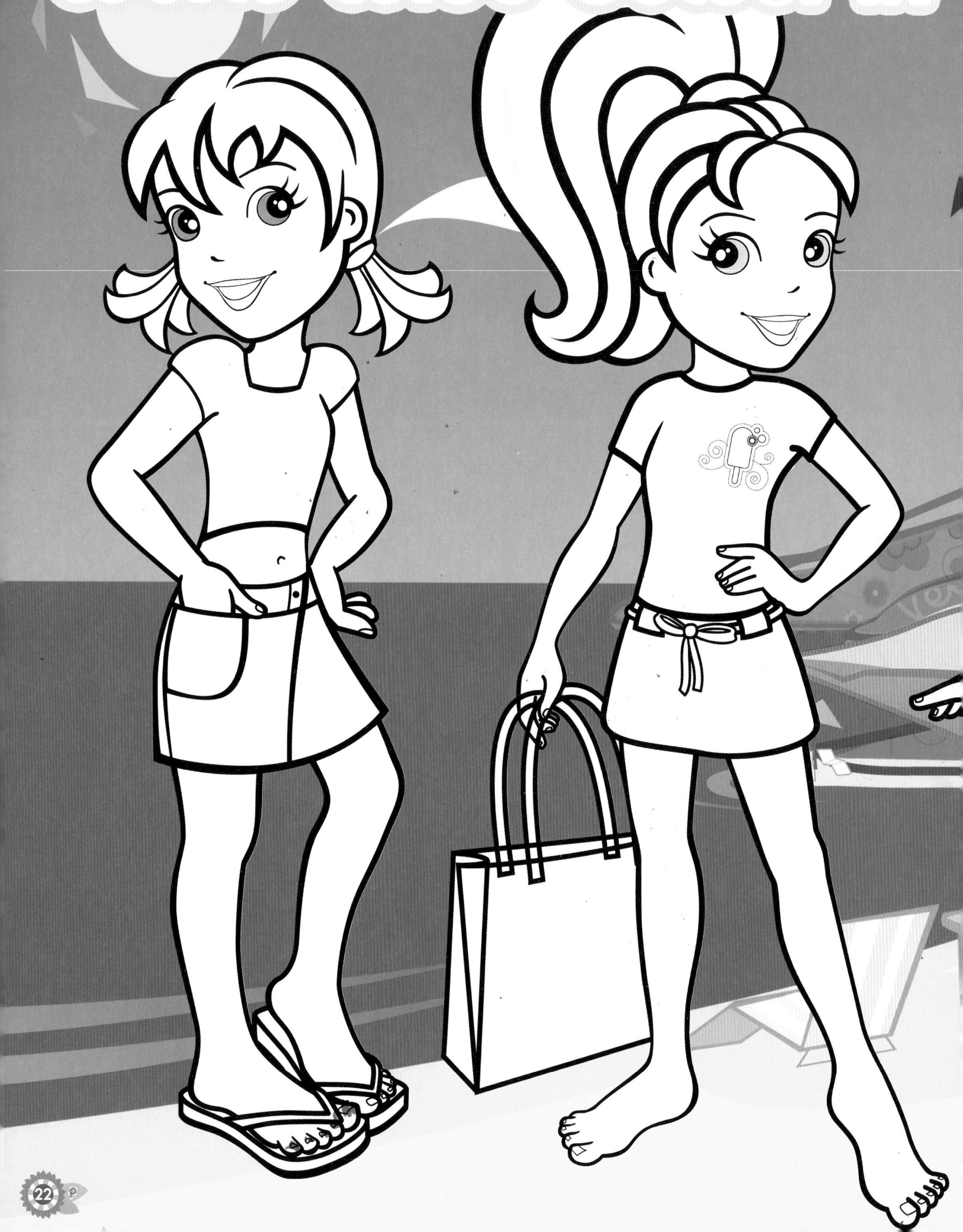

Look at this picture of the girls on holiday. Can you colour them in to make them look as cute and sassy as can be.

23

The Big Polly Wheels Race

Every year at PollyWorld, Mr. Pocket organises a huge race around the park. This year, for the first time, Polly and all her friends were entering. Everyone was going to be there, Lea, Lila, Crissy, Shani and even Rick were all entering their cars. It was going to be a really toptastic day and everyone was looking forward to it, everyone that was, except Lila.

Lila was so nervous about the race that she could hardly think about anything else. She had not been driving for very long and certainly had never been in a race before.

Lila was sometimes not all that confident and so it was good that she had such a great group of friends to support her. She decided to give Polly a call and ask her for some advice.

Lila dialled Polly's number into her phone. "Hi Polly, it's Lila," said Lila. "Hey Lila, how are you?" asked Polly. "Well to be honest I am a little bit worried about the big race tomorrow, I don't think I am going to be any good!" said Lila. "Lila," Polly replied, "Just relax and do your best"
"I'm not really even thinking about winning, I just don't want to come last," said Lila, "Everyone will laugh at me!" "No one is going to laugh at you," said Polly sympathetically, "besides, we think you are super special and super brave for even entering this race!"
"I know you are right," said Lila, "I am just so worried about it."

"Lila, you're a great driver, you have one of the fastest, coolest cars out there and you've got all of us wishing you luck," Polly said reassuringly, "You really do have a chance of winning this race if you just believe in yourself. If you do that then you can do anything!" "Thanks Polly," said Lila, "You always know the right thing to say, you are a totally awesome friend." "Hey Lila, what are friends for" said Polly before saying goodbye and hanging up the phone. Just then, Shani came walking up the street. "Hey honey, how's it going?" asked Shani.

"I have just been talking to Polly about the race tomorrow," said Lila, "I'm a bit worried about it!" "Do you remember the first time I played drums in the band with you?" asked Shani. "Yeah," replied Lila.
"Well I was terrified!" said Shani.
"But, you played despite being scared?"
"Well, that's the thing. I'd been so nervous that I almost didn't go at all!" Eventually Polly talked me into it and I went. I was the first one on stage too!"
"I bet that was scary!" exclaimed Lila.
"It was," replied Shani. "Although, once I'd finished I looked up to see everyone in the crowd and they were all cheering and clapping. They loved it! I 'd been worrying for all that time over absolutely nothing."

"I see! Perhaps I'm worrying about nothing as well then," said Lila as she looked over at her car.

"I'm sure you are, Lila. You'll do just fine. But don't just take it from me, you've got to believe in yourself too, and remember we're all behind you!" said Shani, "Look I have to get going, I've still got to sort my car out for tomorrow, but remember, just believe in yourself, you'll be great! "OK, Shani" Lila shouted after her, "Thanks for your advice!"

Lila started to walk home but she just couldn't get the thought of the race out of her head. On her way back to her house she passed PollyWorld and went in to have a look at the track. There was a race official there putting up a notice about everyone who had entered the race. Lila went to have a look. She already knew that Lea, Polly, Shani, Crissy and Rick were all racing but it turned out that there were another nine cars entered. Some of the names she didn't know but one of them jumped off the page at her...Beth!

Beth had always been very jealous of Polly and all of Polly's friends and bad things always seemed to happen when she was around so you can imagine how worried Lila got when she saw that she would be starting the race right next to her!

"Oh no!" thought Lila, now I really don't have a chance.
Lila continued on her way home and decided to have an early night.

The next morning Lila woke up really early, she had not slept well at all. She had been tossing and turning all night, worrying about the big race that morning. She got up and got dressed, she was still in two minds as to whether she was going to even show up for the race when her phone rang. It was Polly.

"Hi Lila," said Polly, "I was just calling to see how you were feeling and to check you were still coming to the race today.
"Hi Polly," said Lila, "I guess I am coming but yesterday I saw that I was racing against Beth!"
"And?" said Polly
"Well are you not a even a little bit worried about her trying something out on the track?"
"Don't worry Lila," replied Polly, "she is probably just as nervous as you are!"
"Well that's true," said Lila, "hey I'll see you at the track."
"That's stellar supreme," laughed Polly, "I'll see you there.

Lila got into her race suit and headed over to PollyWorld and the race track. Everybody was there, working on their cars and making last minute adjustments.
Beth came over to Lila. She was wearing a very impressive, jet-black race suit with a matching helmet.

"Hi Lila," Beth said with a wry smile, "I'm really looking forward to winning...
I mean racing in this race."
"Me, me too," stammered Lila.
"Are you scared?" asked Beth
"A little," Lila admitted.

"Well you should be," snapped Beth, "You have no chance of beating me, I have the fastest car here and I am by far the best racer at school, so if I were you, I'd just stay out of my way!" Beth turned and marched back to her car. Lila thought to herself for a second. "It's not right of her to talk to me like that, I'll show her!"

"The Race is about to start, could all drivers please get into their cars!" The announcer bellowed over the parks speaker system. Lila ran over to her car but not before wishing good luck to all her friends.
She looked across at Beth who was staring straight at her. Everybody started their engines and sat waiting for the lights to change…

Red. Amber. Green, Go GO GO!

Everybody sped away from the starting line and headed towards the first corner. One car passed Lila and then another and another and another! Soon she found herself at the back of the field, watching all the other cars disappear into the distance.
"Oh no" she said to herself, " I am going to come last!"

Lila kept going, trying to catch up with the others, but however hard she tried, she just couldn't close the gap, in fact, she was falling further and further behind. Lila was about to give up when she suddenly realised something! She had left the handbrake on! No wonder she was going so slowly. She was so nervous that she had made a simple mistake! As she looked up towards the crowd she saw a huge banner that Polly and her pals must have made for her, in big letters it said 'Just believe in yourself, we love you!' Lila thought to herself, if her friends all believed that she could do it, maybe she just had to believe in herself too right?

Lila put the pedal to the metal and had soon caught up with the rest of the pack. She was overtaking one car after another. She could hardly believe it. She was doing so well! Suddenly she found herself in fourth place. She pulled up alongside the car she was trying to overtake and saw that it was Rick.

"Go on Lila, you're too fast for me, show them what you're made of!" he shouted as she sped by!

Lila pulled up in third behind Polly and Beth, there was only one lap left to go now but Lila was so excited, she really looked as though she stood a real chance of winning!

The three front-runners were now all driving side by side.

Just then, Beth looked over at Polly and turned her car towards her sending Polly spinning off the track and onto the soft grass verge.

"Hey!" yelled Lila, "That's cheating!""

"All is fair in love and war," Beth yelled back laughing.

Lila immediately pulled her car onto the side of the track and ran over to check on Polly.

"Polly! Are you alright?" asked Lila with genuine concern.

"I'm fine Lila, why did you stop?" said Polly as she got out of her car.

"I thought you might have been hurt," said Lila.

"Thanks Lila, I'm fine, but my car on the other hand...!" Both girls looked down to see that all of Polly's tyres were flat.

"It's so sweet of you to check on me like that" continued Polly, "but you were in the lead, you could have won the race!"

"Your being ok is way more important to me than any kind of race!" said Lila smiling at Polly.

"Your right," said Polly, "but it is a real shame that you didn't win."
"Polly, if it wasn't for you I wouldn't have even entered the race" said Lila, "Come on let's go and get a soda, this race suit is way too hot, and I have the worst case of helmet hair!"

As Polly and Lila got up and walked to the edge of the track, Beth crossed the finish line and took the chequered flag.
"Well that's just typical," Lila said to Polly.
"Don't worry Lila, cheaters never prosper!"
said Polly smiling at her friend.

A little while later, Mr. Pocket was on the podium awarding the prizes for the race.
"Well, I think it is fair to say that this years race was perhaps the most exciting one we have had yet." Mr. Pocket said. "And the final few laps were very exciting, so exciting that one of our drivers may have got a little carried away out there."
Beth shifted uncomfortably on the podium.
"It is with great regret that I have to inform you that after consulting with our race marshals here today, our winner Beth, has been disqualified."
"What?" yelled Beth as she turned a bright shade of red.
"So," Mr. Pocket continued, "Our winner today who was in second place before stopping to help one of her fellow drivers is…Lila!"
The crowd clapped and cheered as Lila went up onto the podium to collect her trophy.
Lila hushed the crowd.
"I really don't deserve this trophy so I would like to share it will all my friends who gave me the confidence to enter this race. I love all you guys!" Lila yelled as she lifted the trophy above her head.

Flat tyre, GO BACK 3!

Hedgehog crossing, MISS A TURN!

Car breaks down, MISS 2 TURNS!

polly pocket ™

FINISH

spot the difference

Look at these two pictures of Polly and the girls on the dance floor busting some stellar moves. The two pictures might look the same but there are 10 little differences between the two. Can you spot them all?

The Pollytastic Fashion Show

Polly has always known that she is a very lucky young girl, so when she heard that the local kids club was going to shut down because they had run out of money, she just knew that she had to do something about it. Straight away she called all her friends and invited them over to her house to talk about what they could do. Lila was the first to arrive.

"Hi Polly, what's going on, you sounded a bit down on the phone" said Lila as she walked into Polly's bedroom.

"Well," said Polly, "You know how my Dad supports lots of local charities, the Kids Club in town is going to shut down because they have run out of money!"

"Oh no!" cried Lila, "But the local kids love going there after school, there's so much fun stuff for them to do together!"

"Exactly!" said Polly, "We have to do something about this."

Soon, all the rest of the gang arrived and they all sat down to discuss ideas for how they could raise some money. "What about a car wash?" asked Crissy.

"It's a good idea," said Polly but I think we need to think bigger, we have to raise a lot of money." "Ok," said Crissy, "What about a Bus wash?"

The girls giggled. "What about a sponsored walk?" Lea suggested. "It's been done a lot before though," said Polly. "I've got it!" said Lila, "What about a sponsored shopathon?" "Lila, as much as I like that idea, I don't think anyone is going to sponsor us to go shopping," sighed Polly.

"Let's think about what we are good at", said Crissy, "that might help." "Well we could always put on a show with the band," suggested Shani. "But everyone has seen us play so many times, we need something different!" said Polly. "Shopping?" suggested Lila again.

"Lila, you're a genius!" cried Polly. "I was only joking," said Lila. "I know, not shopping but fashion!" cried Polly jumping up and down in excitement, "I don't get it," said Shani looking confused. "What do we know most about?" Polly asked her friends. "Fashion!" all the girls cried together. "Exactly, we'll put on a fashion show at PollyWorld!" yelled Polly.

All the girls got really excited and started jumping around on Polly's bed.

The next day at school, everybody was talking about Polly's big fashion show. Everyone was really excited about it and thought that it was going to be a great fundraiser for the Kids Club Charity. Polly and the gang all met up with each other at lunchtime to talk about their plans. "Right girls," said Polly, "The first thing we need to do is set a date."

"The sooner the better I guess" said Shani, " We really need to get this money to the kids!" "You're right," said Polly, "What about this Saturday?" Everybody was in agreement. "Ok, next we need to make up some posters," said Polly, "Lea, your really good at art, could you do that?" "Sure," replied Lea smiling, "No problem." "Ok then, the rest of us will have to decorate then venue, find some models and find a designer to lend us some clothes!" "Wow! We are going to be busy!" said Lila.

Just then Beth walked by. Beth really didn't get on with Polly and was quite jealous of her popularity. "Oh! What is all this?" she asked looking at their plans. "How cute, you are having a little fashion show!" "It's to raise money for charity," said Lea. "It's to raise money for charity!" mocked Beth, "Well no one is going to go because I have just decided that I am going to be throwing the most fantabulous party ever on Saturday! No one is going to want to go to a boring old fashion show instead of one of my parties!" "You can't do that!" said Lea in a shocked voice, "This is to raise money for some needy kids."

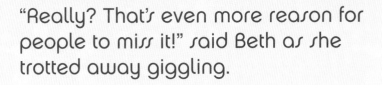

"Really? That's even more reason for people to miss it!" said Beth as she trotted away giggling.

"That's not fair!" said Crissy, "why would she do something so mean?"
"Don't worry about it girls," said Polly, "People will know the right thing to do!" With that the girls got on with their jobs. Lea made some excellent posters that looked totally cool and the rest of the girls sorted out decorations for the venue. Soon it was time to start looking for models. The girls walked around the school asking people if they wanted to take part. Polly even asked Beth if she wanted to be a model, but Beth just ignored her a walked away. Now the only thing they needed to do was find a designer that would provide all the clothes for the show.

"I bet your Dad will know someone Polly!" said Shani. "I bet you're right!" said Polly as she quickly called her Dad. A few moments later Polly got off the phone and turned to her friends.
"You'll never guess who Dad has arranged a meeting for with us?"
"Who?" the girls asked.
"The world famous Italian designer, Franco Muchofussi," cried Polly.
"No way!" screamed the girls as they jumped around in excitement.

The next day the girls were up bright and early and on their way to meet with Franco Muchofussi. They were all a little nervous because Mr. Muchofussi was a very well known designer, who was well known as much for his temper as he was for his clothes. They were all going to meet at the offices in PollyWorld. Polly and the girls arrived and Mr. Muchofussi was already sat at the big long table in Mr. Pocket's office.

"And just where do you think you have been?" he yelled in his strong Italian accent when he saw the girls. "I am very sorry Mr. Muchofussi, I thought we had arranged to meet at 10am?" said Polly. "No, no, no! It was 9:30am! I have been waiting here for half an hour!" Mr. Muchofussi shouted.

Polly looked at the other girls as if to say, 'this is going to be hard work!'

"I am ever so sorry Mr. Muchofussi," said Polly, "It was our mistake, we are so very grateful for you helping us and agreeing to meet with us today, we know how famous you are, and how very busy you must be!" Mr. Muchofussi began to calm down a little. It seemed that he liked to be told how great he was!

"Oh Mr. Muchofussi, I am your biggest fan!" exclaimed Shani. "Well that is understandable!" said Mr. Muchofussi. "We simply love your work and so do all the girls at our school," Lea added. "And everyone we know would love you to come and help us with the fashion show, you are after all the best designer in the world," said Crissy smiling as big a smile as she could manage. "Yes, yes, that is true too!" said Mr. Muchofussi.

"So… do you think you could find it in your heart to help us tomorrow at the fashion show? asked Polly in her sweetest voice. "Okay! I do it!" snapped Mr. Muchofussi, ' But I be there at 6:00am sharp. If you not there, I leave and go back to Milano!" "Thank you so much!" cried the girls as they ran to Mr. Muchofussi to try and give him a hug. "Don'ta touch me!" he yelled, "If you do good tomorrow, then you can'a touch me! With that Mr. Muchofussi stormed out of the office. "Well," said Polly turning to her friends, I think that went well!"
All the girls began to laugh.

It was the morning of the fashion show and all the girls had been there since dawn. The venue looked beautiful with silk and ribbons hanging everywhere. There was a long catwalk where some of models were practicing their walks. Outside there were queues of people waiting to get inside to see all of Mr. Muchofussi's latest designs. Beth was stood across the street watching all of the kids from school waiting to get into the fashion show. "I'll show them," Beth said to herself, "If they're not coming to my party, maybe I'll just make a splash at theirs!"

The show was about to start and Mr. Muchofussi was running around barking out orders to all the models. "You, put this on!" he yelled at one model, "You, don't wear those shoes with that dress! It was chaos! Finally the crowd was allowed into the venue and they took their seats. You could feel the excitement in the air. High above the catwalk, Beth was climbing across the scaffolding that held all the spotlights. She was carrying a big bucket of paint. She wedged the bucket in the lighting rig and tied a piece of string to it before climbing back down and hiding under the stage. "When Polly comes out, she is really going to get a surprise!" Beth giggled to herself.

The show started and the crowd clapped and gasped at all the beautiful clothes that were on show. It was going really well. Polly and her friends all came out together wearing some beautiful dresses and the crowd cheered wildly for them. Beth was under the stage, this was her chance. She yanked on the string, but nothing happened! She pulled harder on it, but again, nothing happened. She got up from under the stage and ran onto the catwalk. "Stop! Stop!" she yelled, "Why are you all not at my party? This thing is totally boring!" Polly picked up a microphone. "Ladies and Gentlemen, let me introduce our final model for this evening... Beth!"

Beth didn't know what to do. She looked quite embarrassed but as the crowd cheered she started strutting up and down the catwalk. Mr. Muchofussi, who had been watching from backstage came storming out shouting " this is not one of my designs, this looksa like a potato sack!" Mr. Muchofussi chased Beth back up the catwalk and caught her at the top. Just as he grabbed her, the bucket of paint fell from the lighting rig and covered them both! The crowd burst into laughter as Beth and Mr. Muchofussi ran backstage desperately trying to get the paint off each other.

Polly and her friends raised enough money to keep the Kids Club open, they raised so much in fact, that the club was able to add an extension to its building and help even more children!

That Fashion Feeling

Polly and the girls,
All have their own sense of style
So just sit back and relax,
And listen for a while.

Shani is really trendy,
Cool and smart and hip,
"Always be individual!"
That would be her tip.

She never really worries
About following the crowd,
She'll wear whatever she feels like
Be it dark, bright or loud.

Then there's sporty Lea,
Who likes to be real comfy,
She's not that happy in a dress,
She'd rather be in Khakis

Lila loves to shop,
She could do it as her profession,
In fact she does it so so much
It's becoming an obsession!

She loves to hit the stores
Especially if there's a sale
And when she sees a bargain
She'll grab it without fail.

Polly loves clothes too,
She's really into fashion,
In fact you might even say
It's one of her biggest passions.

But Polly knows it's not
about clothes,
It's what is on the inside,
Because even with the
nicest clothes,
Your true self you
cannot hide!

Polly's Pet Maze

Polly's Pictures

Polly just loves taking photos of her friends, she has taken some super close-ups and is a little bit confused who is who... Can you guess who each photo is of and write it down so Polly knows?

① lila

② lea

③ Shani

④ Crissy

Polly's Pet Pickle

Polly and her friends have been having a pool party and while they were busy splashing about and having fun some of Polly's pets have gotten into the loby. Can you find a parrot, a kitten, a puppy, a bunny, a leopard cub and a husky puppy? Look very carefully because they are very good at hiding.

Kitty Cat Conundrum

Can you help the poor little kitty cat find her way through the maze to her bed, she'll love you forever if you can!

Perfect Puppy Pairs

Look at the pictures of the cute little puppy below, can you spot the two pictures that are the same?

Perfectly Pretty Pets

Why don't you help Polly make her little puppy and her cute kitten look even more pretty for the PollyWorld Pet-show. Use your crayons to colour in these two pictures and and make them as cute as can be!

PollyWorld Safari

Polly and her friends
Love to go to Polly's Zoo
It's actually a safari,
Would you like to come to?

Lea loves the Parrots
Because of their bright looks
She could sit and draw them all day
And fill all of her sketch books.

She also likes the zebra's,
Because they run around and play.
Just like Lea, they're never bored
Of being outside all day.

Shani likes the gibbons,
Because their walk is really funky,
She thinks it's like they're dancing,
They're her favourite kind of monkey!

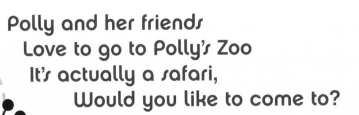

Lila likes the flamingos,
    Because they look pretty in pink.
        She'd like to take one out shopping,
        I don't know, what do you think?

      Rick, he likes the rhinos,
        They are big and strong and tough,
      He could watch them forever,
      And never have had enough.

Polly loves all the animals,
    Big and tall or short and plump.
    But she really likes the Kangaroos
Especially how they jump.

    Everyone loves the Safari Park,
  Watching the animals roam free.
"Polly, next time you go,
Will you please take me?"

Pick Polly An Outfit

Polly loves to try on all different kinds of clothes. Look at her here on these two pages, which outfit do you think looks the best? Colour in all the clothes...

Polly's Perfect Picture

Polly and the gang had this photo taken on their last holiday. Can you find all of the items listed below in the picture?

All the gang are here to wave goodbye! Can you colour them all in using your crayons. Try to stay in the lines and make the picture perfect!

Answers

Page 34 *Spot the Difference*

Page 46
Polly's Pet Maze

1. Lila needs the purple lead.
2. Lea needs the pink lead.
3. Shani needs the orange lead.
4. Polly needs the green lead.

Page 47
Polly's Pictures

1. Lila.
2. Lea.
3. Shani.
4. Crissy.

polly™

polly™